W9-AEW-276

CAESAR

CAESAR

The Life Story of a Panda Leopard

PATRICK O'BRIAN

W. W. NORTON & COMPANY
NEW YORK LONDON

Printed in the United States of America

Manufacturing by The Haddon Craftsmen, Inc.

ISBN 0-393-04918-3

W. W. Norton & Company, Inc., 500 Fifth Avenue, New York, N.Y. 10110
www.wwnorton.com

W. W. Norton & Company Ltd., 10 Coptic Street, London WC1A 1PU

1 2 3 4 5 6 7 8 9 0

FOREWORD

IT IS A CURIOUS EXPERIENCE, looking back from a distance of more than seventy years at the little creature who shared one's name, bones, and indeed a good deal of one's essential being, as far as it can be made out at all objectively. Curious and by no means entirely agreeable: I doubt if my present self would have liked the twelve-year-old boy who wrote this tale – he was certainly not very popular among his brothers and sisters. Nevertheless, that remote being and myself, his aged descendant, are linked by a common delight in reading: the boy read voraciously, often in bed, by the light of an electric torch. And when he was very young his stepmother, the kindest of women, took him to see her sister, who gave him the Reverend Mr Wood's *Natural History,* a mid-nineteenth-century edition illustrated with a fair number of engravings. Since he was already something of a naturalist (an admired, much older brother had practically invented birds), the boy devoured the book, which was written by a sensible, well-informed, scholarly man. The boy was also something of an invalid, which interfered with his education and worried his father, a bacteriologist in the early days of vaccines and electrical treatment: the young fellow (pre-adolescent: a sort of elderly child) therefore spent long sessions in the incubator room, sitting at a glass-topped metal table and doing the simple tasks set by his tutor. But the tasks left a good deal of time unoccupied, and since it was obviously unthinkable to bring a book to read, the boy, by some mental process that I can no longer recall, decided to write one for himself, thus discovering an extraordinary joy which has never left him – that of both reading and writing at the same time.

It may seem absurd and pretentious, above all apropos of this piece of juvenilia, to say that writers, once they have experienced this intense delight, live fully only when they are writing fast, at the top of their being: the rest of the time only the lacklustre shell of the man is present, often ill-tempered (deprived of his drug), rarely good company.

Patrick O'Brian
Trinity College, Dublin 1999

CAESAR

ONE

FIRST you must understand that I am a panda-leopard. My father was a giant panda and my mother a snow-leopard.

I will begin my story at the first things that I can remember.

My early days were spent with two brothers and a sister in a large cave, high up in the side of a mountain.

Of my father I remember little, except a hazy recollection of a very large shape which brought food to my mother in the first few days of the opening of my eyes.

The first thing to make any great impression on my mind was the killing of my sister.

It happened like this – the day was very cold, we were huddled together for warmth, and mother had gone for food, when I heard a scratching noise outside, and somehow it frightened us, for the others had heard it too.

Then a head appeared in the mouth of the cave. It was that of a large black bear.

The face seemed to split almost in half as the bear roared, and this sent us into the back of the cave, all except my sister, who sat petrified with fear in the middle of the floor.

The bear came right into the cave, and then shot out one of his great paws, and struck her a blow which laid her dead at our feet.

Then he picked her up and went out growling terribly.

Scarcely had the bear gone, when mother returned carrying a tough old pig.

She smelt around for a little, and seemed worried. Then she noticed my sister's absence, and with a low growl she went straight out of the cave, following the tracks of the bear.

She came back late in the evening with her white fur splashed with blood, both her own and the bear's, and in her mouth she carried two bear cubs, both quite dead. She was very tired as she had kept up a running fight for miles before they had reached the bear's lair, where mother had killed him.

We ate the bear cubs.

Next day passed uneventfully, but I missed my sister in a dim sort of way. We played as usual, but I noticed that one of my brothers stayed out of our games and seemed unhappy.

As the night approached he was more uneasy, and mother licked him to soothe his whimpering, and this calmed him; but by nightfall he was howling and crying, as if in pain, and mother looked anxious.

We tried to make him play, but he just sat still, not even retaliating when I bit his tail.

Soon after this I went to sleep, as there was no fun to be got out of him.

Next morning we found that he was gone, and we saw by his tracks that he had gone straight out of the cave, down the mountain-side and over the frozen stream at its foot. Here we saw the signs of a struggle. A hyena had got him.

Two or three weeks passed quite happily, but the snow did not melt, and food was getting rather scarce, and then one day mother took us out to hunt.

We went down the mountain-side and on to the stream which was still frozen stiff, and here my brother and I slipped and fell many times before mother showed us how to walk on ice.

On the other side we rested, for our little legs soon got tired, and then we went on again.

A snow-hare jumped up about ten yards away, and I, wildly excited, set off after it, but the next moment I received a cuff on the side of the head that sent me sprawling as mother shot by me after the hare. She secured it in a few seconds, and we ate it where we were, as it was only a small one.

As we were eating it I took my little piece behind a fallen bough, and after I had finished it I looked at the branch more closely.

I poked it and rolled it over, and then all at once a lot of bees came buzzing out. One stung me on the nose, and I fled howling dolefully to mother.

She licked the place, but she did not seem to think, as I did, that I was in any immediate danger of death.

Soon after this incident we went home, as my brother and I were quite tired out by our exertions, which chiefly consisted of getting in the way and eating the food which mother had killed.

About a month passed before anything happened. We were quite well and growing very fast, when my brother began to behave rather strangely, and his moping put me in mind of my other brother, who had run away a long time before.

One afternoon when I was teasing him to make him play, I received a blow from mother that sent me sulking into a corner for the rest of the day.

This seemed to cheer my brother somewhat, and he ate a little piece of the goat which mother brought in that night. After this he made one attempt to run away, but mother brought him back before he had got beyond the stream, which had thawed.

Next day mother brought in two little grey apes which we ate, but they did not agree with me, however, as I had horrible dreams all through the night. I have never eaten apes since.

On the following morning my brother was sick, and after this he got rapidly well again, being a strongly constituted young animal.

I awoke rather late in the day and found that mother had gone out, my brother killed a mouse and was immensely proud of it. I thought that it must have been both blind and paralysed, but it made no difference to his pride.

Mother soon returned, carrying with her a sambhur faun, and we ate some of it. Then mother took us out for exercise. We took the same path as before, but almost immediately after stepping out of the cave I missed my footing and started to roll down the slope, gathering speed as I went, but mother caught me before I had rolled any distance, and set me on my feet. I was quite giddy and sorry for myself, so when my brother suddenly pushed me from behind, I tripped and started rolling off towards the stream, into which I fell with a loud splash. As all the ice had melted I found nothing to hold on to, but instinct made me strike out – but not, however, before I had consumed what seemed half the water in the stream.

I swam towards the opposite bank, but the current washed me out into mid-stream and I went under again. Then I heard a splash behind me, as mother jumped in.

She soon had me by the scruff of the neck and swam ashore with a few powerful strokes. Once on dry land she shook all the water out of her fur, and I copied her. Then we trotted down the stream, and as we went I wondered why water was so wet, and why one could not breathe in it. Also why it was cold and unpleasant. I was very puzzled by the time we reached the ford, where mother stopped and walked in. It only reached to the top of her legs in the middle, so I plucked up my courage and followed her. Looking round I saw that my brother would not come in, so when mother and I had got to the other side and walked up the bank, she went back through the water, and taking him by the loose skin on the back of his neck, she carried him in; but when she had got to mid-stream, she lowered him in and he gave a dismal howl, which, however, was choked by water.

After this, he kept his head above the water and walked with her. As he scrambled up the bank, I remembered how he had pushed me down the slope, and I knocked him back again. He soon scrambled out, and after mother had licked us we set off again into the forest, mother leading the way.

We went in single file, mother leading; and my brother kept nipping my tail until we came to an opening in the trees, where I fell upon him and mother separated us.

She showed us a lot of short, cropped grass in the clearing, and taught us that it had been eaten by deer. Then she showed us a little piece of fur on a thorn, which she made us smell and taught us that this was the smell of sambhur. We found the trail, and here and there a little fresh-cropped grass. After we had followed this trail for about a quarter of a mile into the forest we saw a cross track, a lot of little double-pointed footprints, which smelt different from deer. Very silently we followed the trail, which was quite fresh. The trails crossed and inter-crossed it, but the peculiar scent always distinguished it.

At last we came to a big, muddy clearing where a sounder of wild pigs – as a large family is called – was feeding. The sentinel pig saw us, and gave the alarm. The sounder fled at once, but with one bound mother caught up a little sucking-pig, and tossing it into the air she broke its neck. She picked it up in her mouth and began to go home. I very much wanted to chase the pigs, but it was not to be: I got a few steps after them, when mother picked me up and drove me in front of her. When we reached the ford, mother carried us over, as we were very small and tired.

When we got home we just had the energy to consume the pig, and then my brother and I went fast asleep.

TWO

ABOUT one month later I saw my first human being. Mother had taken us out as usual, but we returned rather late. Imagine our surprise when we saw five things that looked like big apes in our cave, all gathered round something that was smoking and smelling under a lot of sticks. I did not understand it, but I feared the smoky thing, instinctively. The effect it had on my mother was extraordinary. She crouched on the ground with her ears flattened back and her tail twitching. She was growling terribly.

Then instead of charging the apes (humans) as I fully expected, she turned round and went down towards the stream. We followed her, and together we went upstream away from the ford; and soon we found ourselves at the mouth of another cave in the side of the bank of the stream, which had cut itself very deep.

Here we halted and mother went into the cave. I heard a roar, followed by the sound as of a scuffle, and two jackals shot out howling. Then we went in, and after snuggling down in the dried fern in the back of the cave we went to sleep.

At about midnight I awoke shivering. I heard mother growl uneasily, then the wind blew into the cave and I knew why I had awakened. It was the smell of fire. My brother soon awoke, and together we left the cave. All the forest on our left was blazing, and behind us and on our right the shrubs and long grass were burning furiously. The fire which the humans had made had spread and caught the trees. The only thing to do was to run south. So we ran.

After about five minutes we had caught up and passed many animals. There was a family of wild pigs led by a splendid old boar, and many goats who had come down in the evening to drink at the stream, and who had been caught by a wing of the fire.

We also passed two leopards, innumerable rats and mice and one old bear. How many animals there were to the left and right of us and in front I would not care to say, but there must have been thousands.

At last we found ourselves well in the van, the only beasts in front were the deer. Then my brother stepped on a porcupine, and filled his paws with quills. The startled beast lashed out with its long tail, filling my flank with the sharp points. We waited while we got most of them out.

But meanwhile the fire was fast overtaking us. About half a mile in front of us could be seen the waters of a lake shimmering in the moonlight. Not a large lake, but big enough to stop the fire. If only we could get there we would be safe.

Many animals were in the water already, but there was room for hundreds more. We put on an extra spurt, but we cubs were very tired and were getting rather too large for mother to carry. Soon the sparks were falling on us, and I felt almost suffocated by the smoke. My brother stumbled and fell, I ran on but mother stayed and lifted him, then I turned and between us we got him nearly to the lake.

By now the trees were burning all around us, and with a crash a burning pine-tree came down. I had barely time to leap for my life when another fell across my mother's back, pinning her down. Then the fire swept over them, and I was forced into the lake.

THREE

AFTER the death of my mother I naturally had to fend for myself. Of course, mother had shown me how to kill and how to hunt properly, so I managed fairly well for some time.

At first I only got rats and small deer. I also put up with lizards, but soon all food became very scarce as all the grass for the game had been burnt by the fire.

At first the larger animals moved south, and after them all the smaller ones, the process being gradual; but in about three weeks I decided to change my quarters, so early one morning I set off up the stream. After following it for five miles I found myself going up a considerable hill. At last I got to the top, and there I saw a large plateau stretching in a grassy plain in a circle of about three miles in diameter. Here I saw no traces of the fire whatever. But in about the centre of the plain I saw a number of things that resembled very large boulders, and there were creatures moving around them. Then the wind veered in my direction and blew their scent towards me, and I knew that they were men. I also caught the scent of goats and pigs, and I saw that there was a large herd of them in a small copse of trees about a quarter of a mile away.

As the wind was favourable I approached them, taking advantage of all the cover there was. I had very little difficulty in getting quite close. Then to my dismay I saw that there was a man with them.

Being very hungry I decided to take a risk, and as a small pig came unsuspectingly almost to my nose, I sprang on to his back, breaking his neck. Unluckily, the pig had time to squeal, and this attracted the man who, with a cry, picked up a stone. His arm went back and the stone flew towards me like a bird. It hit me on the nose and hurt me more than the bee-sting which I had had when a cub. It hit me on the same tender place which had never quite got better, and it angered me beyond words, and dropping the pig I charged, running low along the ground. Then I sprang straight at him.

With a shriek of fear he struck at me with a stick, and missed. We fell together, but his skull was cracked like an egg-shell. It was ridiculously easy to kill him.

Then something inside me made me want to roar, and tell the world that I had killed a man. So I roared for the first time. I was almost frightened at the sound I made, and the effect I made on the pigs and goats who had not already disappeared was magical. They ran for the boulders like the wind, and I never thought there was such speed in a pig until I saw them run that day. It was wonderful.

Then I looked down at the man. He had the strangest skin I had ever seen. It was loose and of all colours. Later I got to know that they were clothes, but at the time I was puzzled. He also smelt very strongly, so I left him and went to seek the pig which also smelt of men, but not so badly.

But I was hungry and made no bones about it. I dragged it under a bush and made a good meal, but before I had got half-way through the pig I observed a number of men coming out of the huts – for such were the boulders. It was evident that they were coming to investigate the cause of the sudden return of the flocks.

I saw that they were too many for me to deal with, so dragging the pig into some bushes, I made for a cluster of rocks which would hide me and yet allow me to see what was going on. Once among the rocks I was quite safe, for my coat matched the dull grey perfectly, so I lay in a sort of natural tunnel in which I was invisible. But through a small hole in the farther end I could see what was happening.

The men approached the body of the herdsman, which I had forgotten to hide. This seemed to anger them, and then they examined my tracks, and one old man, a hunter I believe, followed them as far as the place where I had left the pig. It was plain that these men were very foolish, for the wind was blowing from me to them. And if they had had any sense at all they would have smelt me at once.

They found the pig, or rather half of it, and set up a chattering like a lot of frenzied monkeys. They appeared more concerned about the pig than about the man.

Then they held a consultation like I have seen the monkeys do, all speaking at once.

Finally, however, two of them ran back to the village, and after about five minutes returned with five large animals that looked rather like wolves – I found out later they were dogs. The creatures were led to the place where the pig had been found, and they then picked up my track.

Slowly but surely they got nearer and nearer to my retreat, until they reached the first of the rocks. When they got as far as this I turned round in the tunnel and charged out. I took them by surprise, killing one dog and scattering the rest.

Once past the dogs it was plain sailing, for none of the men cared to follow me, even if they could. The dogs pursued me but had little chance of catching me, for though they could run nearly as fast as I, they could not keep it up. I shook off the dogs in about a quarter of an hour, all except one which was of a different breed from the rest, having longer legs and a slimmer body. After running at a breakneck speed for about four minutes, I suddenly leaped into the air, and on landing spread out all my feet and stopped suddenly. The dog could not stop and went careering on in front of me. Then in a few moments I had him pinned down, and despatched him at once. Then I made for the stream to put off the scent, and swam awkwardly down it for a little way.

On getting out I decided to go back to the old cave where I was born, but on reflection I thought that the cave in the side of the bank was more comfortable and nearer the herds. I went towards it, but I had forgotten the jackals who lived there, so I got a shock when on entry they mistook me for something small and set upon me. They soon discovered their mistake, however.

One fled for the stream, and reaching the bank he could not stop and plunged right in, nearly getting drowned. The other got his neck in the way of my teeth, so he made no more mistakes.

That night I slept well, but I woke feeling very hungry, and I thought of going up to the village again; but on reflection I decided not to, as they were sure to be waiting for me. So I decided to go up the mountain, where I knew there were plenty of ibex to be found, and also mountain sheep.

On my way up I passed the old cave. About three hundred feet above the cave the grass ended. Then I was in the part of the mountain which the ibex favoured, where I saw the tracks of a troop of about twenty of them. The tracks led upwards, and soon I found myself in the region where the snow began. I was on a ledge between a sheer face of rock and a drop of six hundred feet, a ledge about a yard wide between the bare rock and destruction. After I had got about one hundred yards, a part of the ledge on which my two hind legs had been resting gave way, and I had barely time to jump forward when about six feet of the thin ledge behind me fell down with a terrific crash.

Now it was impossible for me to go back, as I dare not try to jump, so I went on along the ledge. Soon I came to a corner, and round it I thought I saw one of the ibex disappear. The ledge became a little wider, so I put on a spurt, and rounding the corner I came face to face with a man.

FOUR

THE first to recover was the ibex, who turned and bolted towards the man, going straight between his legs. The man quickly recovered, and stood staring at me in terror. We stood thus for fully ten seconds, when an eagle above us screamed. The man started and looked up.

I saw my opportunity and took it. He only looked up for about a second, but I had time to knock him over the edge, and he went scrambling over the side. As he fell he threw out his arms and obtained a grip on the ledge, and there he hung.

Slowly the fingers began to slip, then his right hand lost its hold. His face assumed a horrible expression, and with a despairing cry he slipped, and when I looked over I could only see a heap, which didn't move.

Then, feeling rather sick, I followed the ledge along and at last came out on a high, bare plain, which was just below the region of snow, where a flock of mountain goats were feeding on the sparse vegetation.

I took advantage of all the cover that there was, but the goats were up-wind of me, so they got my scent before I had time to get very near. The sentinel gave the alarm, and off they went like the wind, going straight up the mountain-side on to the rocks that I couldn't reach. I caught a kid, however, and picking it up started the return journey. Before I had gone one hundred yards, however, I felt something like a sharp-pointed thunderbolt in my rear quarters. I turned to face this new enemy, and I saw that it was the kid's mother.

Dropping the kid I awaited the attack of the furious goat. I knew how strong the mother-love was in goats, so I knew that she would fight to the end.

She charged with her long horns lowered. I darted to one side, and with my paw I got in a blow which ripped her open to the shoulder-bone. Then wonderfully quickly she turned and gored me in the side. I leaped clear, and we stood panting and looking at each other for a second. Then I charged, and leaping on to her back I broke her neck.

Then I took up the kid again, and set off home, but by another route. On my way I found my wound was beginning to hurt, so I rested and licked it awhile, thinking as I did so that it was rather curious that I should be wounded by a goat.

I did not notice, however, that the sky was rapidly darkening, so when I started again I had to hurry, for I knew there was about to be a storm. Everything was very quiet, and I was vaguely alarmed, for I had not experienced anything like it before.

Then a cold wind began to hum through the pines, and I began to run as fast as I possibly could towards home. The pain in my side increased, and so did my terror, when I suddenly came within sight of the old cave. Then the storm broke with a blinding flash of lightning and a formidable roll of thunder.

I was not more than twenty yards from the cave, but I was soaked through before reaching it. In the cave I found three hares and a faun, which all darted out when they saw me. Then I lay down and watched the storm.

That night I was lulled to sleep by the swish of the rain, which came down in sheets. When I awoke in the morning it was coming down as hard as ever; the dark sky was lighted by flashes of lightning, and the stream below was converted into a broad, roaring torrent.

I felt very hungry, and then I remembered the kid which I had put in the back of the cave. I dragged it out and made a good meal. He was very tender, if a little stale.

Then for the rest of the day I licked myself until my fur shone. There was nothing else to do except watch the rain. As the day wore on the lightning and thunder became worse, and several trees were struck. Forked lightning was particularly beautiful, as it played almost incessantly.

The night passed uneventfully. But in the morning I noticed that the stream was swollen to five times its previous size, and every now and then drowned animals floated down. I felt very unwell on account of my wound, which I could not easily get at to lick, and it had begun to fester and throb painfully.

Then suddenly the rain stopped, and there was silence like that which preceded the storm. Soon I heard noises as of animals and birds beginning to move again, and I got up to go down to the stream. Before I had gone far, however, my wound and my weakness through lack of food forced me to stop, and I lay down quite dizzy.

I soon was able to get up and go to the stream, which was very swollen. Here and there on the banks I could see drowned animals, such as goats, pigs and small deer, on whose dead bodies a number of jackals and hyenas were already feeding. But they fled on my approach.

I had a drink and felt better for it. Then as evening was coming on I ensconced myself in a heap of debris which had been washed down, in the hope that some deer or goats might come down to drink. My hopes were fulfilled before I expected, for no sooner had I hidden myself when a half- grown sambhur arrived. It had got separated from its mother in the storm.

I crept up behind it quietly, but it saw me, so I had to charge quickly. I broke its neck quite easily, but my wound had torn open, and I crept back to my shelter carrying the sambhur and bleeding profusely. I lay down for some time, very weak for want of food and loss of blood, and felt very dizzy and soon went into a kind of sleep. I dreamt for the first time. My dream was about the fire in which my mother perished, and I saw her quite plainly just before the pine killed her, and I felt very sad.

I woke with a start, and I observed several jackals in front of my shelter waiting for a chance to snatch my kill. They retreated hurriedly when I got up, but to prevent them taking it when I slept I made a meal there and then, and took the rest up to the cave.

My wound had closed, but I knew that any sharp turn or jerk would bring it open again, so I took quite a long time getting up there. I felt strangely weak and shaky about the legs, and I thought I was going to die. But after finishing the sambhur and having a good rest I felt much better, and next morning I was quite myself again.

I went down to the stream, which had subsided a great deal, and had a drink, which was against my usual custom, for I nearly always drank in the evening like the other animals. But the loss of blood had made me thirsty. After that I wandered down to the ford, which I could not wade as usual, so I swam it.

To my no little amazement, I found that if I kept my body under the water instead of trying to leap out after each successive stroke, I could swim quite well without much effort.

On reaching the opposite bank I struck into the forest, and wandered rather aimlessly away from my usual haunts. By noon I had gone farther than I had ever gone before, and when the sun became too oppressive I ascended a tree and rested in the crotch, about twenty-five feet from the ground; and I watched the insects and animals settling down for the midday siesta.

The monkeys made quite a noise for some time, even after the buzz of the mosquitoes had died down. Soon, however, everything was quiet, and I slept with the rest.

FIVE

I WAS awakened suddenly by a stinging pain in the tip of my tail, which I switched up with a start.

Looking down I saw a large party of ants crawling up the bole of the tree, and the front ones had just reached my tail. They covered the whole of the front of the tree in a crawling mass, but in orderly ranks, guarded by warrior ants on either side, in the front and at the back. These warriors had very large jaws, out of all proportion to their size, and one of them was biting me. I whisked it off and went farther up the tree. Soon, however, the ants reached me again, and I went higher this time accompanied by four frightened monkeys and two small pythons.

The behaviour of these beasts reminded me of the way the animals acted when running from the forest fire. As a rule the pythons would have taken the opportunity of a meal in the form of the monkeys, to which they are particularly partial. However, they just ascended the tree in a panic-stricken sort of fashion.

Then one of the snakes half slipped on a rotten branch, and did not recover till he had fallen nearly three feet. He fell in among the front ranks of the ants. In a moment he was covered with them. They swarmed over his body; he opened his mouth to hiss, and they poured down his throat. They bit away his eye-coverings and blinded him, and before two minutes had passed they had killed him and were taking him away in small sections to their nest.

When they had gone I thankfully descended. I could have gone no higher as the branches were getting thinner, and they would soon have broken beneath my weight.

Having descended I made a bee-line towards the village, as I was feeling too lazy to track deer. In about two hours I reached the edge of the plateau. The flocks were there just the same, but there were six men also.

Stealing up to the edge of the herd, I sprang up a tree with low-spreading branches. The leaves afforded excellent cover and shade, and I remained there unobserved for some time, awaiting my chance for an easy kill.

After half an hour had passed I dozed off to sleep. In a few minutes I was awakened by the sound of humans chattering below, one of whom was pointing to my tail, which I had allowed to drop during my sleep so that it hung down through the branches.

The chattering ceased and one of the men took a bright kind of stick, and resting it on his shoulder pointed it at me. Then there was a tremendous report and a flash of fire which frightened me so that I nearly lost my balance, and then something terribly hot hit me in the shoulder, making a searing gash right to my shoulder-blade.

After that I remember nothing but a blind, unreasoning wave of fury which overcame me, and confused shouts – and my claws and teeth sank again and again in human flesh.

When I calmed down enough to stop the useless killing, I found myself alone covered with blood, with two dead men. I dimly felt sorry that I had needlessly killed these two useless things, for though I was hungry I could not bring myself to eat these smelly men.

I went to a small pond in the wood and had a drink. All the animals had disappeared, so I went downstream, homeward. On the way I was lucky enough to see a small pig which had wandered from the main herd. Fat and well fed, the pig could not run like a wild one, so I caught it with great ease.

I reached home, and while I was washing myself preparatory to eating the pig, I found that I had a large cut on my back, evidently from one of the sharp, shiny things which the men carried. It was not deep, however, and healed in a day or two. The pig, as I have said before, was fat and well fed – so I slept well. For three days I laid up in the cave, contenting myself with small deer that came down every evening to drink at the stream.

In this way I soon got over my wound, except for the old wound in my shoulder which left a permanent scar. I avoided the plateau for about fifteen days, but on the sixteenth I went up to the edge of the plain, and lying down in the rocks I formed a plan. After about a quarter of an hour I circled round the herds – always keeping up-wind of them, until I was within a furlong of the village itself, when I advanced towards the track which they always followed when going into the village. Here I concealed myself in some dense brushwood – awaiting their return.

My plan was this – when they were half way past me, I would spring out roaring, and in the confusion disappear with a buffalo calf, if I could get one, or at the worst a large pig.

I had not long to wait, and soon the foremost horned sheep passed me – but I let them go. Soon the men came, but they did not notice that the pigs and goats seemed a little frightened when they passed me. But the wind was blowing well in my direction, so they did not bolt or give notice that they sensed that I was around.

Soon, however, the pigs and sheep had all passed, and then the great water-buffaloes came by – first the bulls with their great needle-pointed curved horns and wicked-looking red eyes. I did not venture to pull one of these giants down in the sight of the rest.

For though the bulls might have stampeded, the cows would have killed me in an instant, for a buffalo cow with calf is easily the most dangerous beast in my fancy. So I changed my plan and waited for the stragglers.

The main body soon passed, and the stragglers began to arrive. I selected a half-grown bull buffalo and charged – roaring. In an instant all was pandemonium, and the main herd stampeded towards the village, which was what I wanted.

The calf seemed petrified with fear, and I sprang on to its shoulders, and in a moment my teeth had met in the back of his neck.

He fell, but from behind some bushes a small cow buffalo – his mother – came charging. I stood my ground over the little buffalo, being furious at my mistake.

When she was about six feet off I sprang, but not high enough, and she got in a blow with her horns which sent me three feet in the air. Luckily the points missed me, and I twisted in the air and fell on her back, and there I stayed. She dashed through the bushes trying to dislodge me, but I stuck on.

Soon, however, the loss of blood which was streaming from her sides weakened her, and as she slowed up I broke her neck, and she fell with a crash.

Slowly and stiffly I got up; my claws seemed on fire from the strain they had endured, and my back was scarred by the marks from branches.

Looking around I saw that we had left the village far behind, and I was near the great pile of rocks where I had been tracked by the dogs before.

I tried to drag my kill towards them, but I quickly realised that she was too heavy for me. I dragged her a little way, but after twenty yards I had to desist. Then taking her up again I succeeded in getting her to the rocks. The great weight was a reminder that I was not yet fully grown, for I remembered seeing my mother carrying a big buck sambhur with ease.

Once in the rocks I made a good meal, for I knew there was no time to lose. Running back after about half an hour, I picked up the little buffalo.

In the village fires were flaring and a terrific hubbub was going on. Taking it by the neck in my mouth and slinging the body over my shoulder, I set off at a rapid trot for home.

This time I did not attempt to cover my tracks by plunging into the stream.

Far behind me I heard the baying of the dogs, but soon I came to the rocky foot of the mountain, which I knew would leave no tracks.

Gaining home, I slept almost at once.

Next morning I wandered off towards the south until noon, when I slept as usual. Instead of a tree, however, I selected a broad slab of rock over a small stream – overhung by the branches of an aspen. Being tired I slept on and on, little suspecting the danger beneath me.

SIX

I AWOKE with a start fairly late in the afternoon, with a sense of danger near me. Seeing nothing, I began to stretch myself and wash.

But I was interrupted by a low hiss, and turning I looked into the face of a large king cobra, which was coiled for a spring, not at me, however, but at something behind me, and towards the left.

Turning sharply, I saw a little brown man crouched like a monkey in some long grass. Then the cobra struck, its head shooting over my tail like a whip-lash. It missed, for the man had dodged to one side and had hit it on the back of the head with a bent stick, and the snake lay motionless on the ground.

All this only took about half a minute, however, but I had time to back out without being seen, for I had never seen any animal like this who could dodge the fastest thing in the jungle.

From my place up a tree which I climbed, I saw him follow my tracks round the rock towards me. Then I lost sight of him, but feeling uneasy I left my tree and concealed myself in the rushes.

Soon I saw him come out of the brushwood, bent double and staring around him. Then he saw a place where I had put my foot in a little patch of mud. He ran to it, and after inspecting it some time he rose with a little whistle of surprise, and disappeared again in the bushes.

Soon after that I came out, feeling hungry. As I have said before, the rock on which I had been lying was over a small pool, and now as it was evening I hoped that some game might come down to drink. So, hiding near the banks, I waited.

In about half an hour there came a sounder of pigs led by a vast boar. Having had some little experience of these boars I knew that it would be better not to touch him or his family, so I let them alone.

Then the pigs began to drink. A few minutes passed, and with a roar a large tiger leapt out of the bushes opposite to me, and the pigs scattered.

One little one ran straight to me, and I secured it without any noise. All the pigs fled except the boar, who stood facing the tiger who, after circling around for a moment, charged.

The boar with great speed leaped to one side, at the same time getting in a blow with his long tusks which opened up the skin from the tiger's shoulder to half way down the ribs. Then before he could recover the boar had swung round and gored him again.

The tiger roared and began to circle round slowly and cautiously – and then he leapt. The boar was too slow, and lost part of his right shoulder. The tiger retreated and continued these tactics for some time, circling and dashing in and back again.

After a while the boar was a sorry sight; all his head and shoulders were bleeding and the blood obscured his vision.

The tiger suddenly leapt in again, but he over-reached himself, missing his mark as he struck, and the boar, with a grunt, lowered his head, and with lightning speed ripped up the tiger.

As he fell, the boar with one great raking thrust completely disembowelled his adversary, who lay kicking on the ground. The boar drew off and soon the tiger's struggles ceased and he lay dead.

Then the boar crawled away into the bushes opposite me, and soon after I saw two jackals near the place. In a few moments five more had come, and from the sky the vultures and crows were coming.

Soon I had finished my pig, and I walked out into the open.

As soon as they saw me the cloud of crows and vultures rose and settled on all the trees around. I looked at the tiger's body and saw beside the main wounds innumerable others all over him.

Having inspected the tiger I went farther south on the trail of some deer. I followed this trail along through what seemed like a beaten track or path until I came to a kind of cross-roads, where another set of deer tracks converged on to the main one. Further along still, I found some more which led into it, and I could tell by the scent that I was coming near to the deer.

Then quite suddenly the sun set and the afterglow set in, and after about five minutes the darkness began to close in.

A month ago I would have been looking for a sleeping-place, but now, oddly enough, I took little notice, for I was growing up and knew that the hunting time for the big carnivores is the night.

I saw the fireflies dancing in among the grasses in front of me, and vaguely I wondered where they got the light from. As I travelled along the deer trails I began to notice a scent in the air which I did not recognise, and as I progressed the smell grew more powerful, until at last I knew I must be very near the beast, whatever it was.

Then breaking through some bushes (I had left the path in my curiosity) I emerged into a clearance, where I saw a huge black shape standing still in a corner.

It was an elephant, and what is more it was a rogue elephant, or a mad one which had been driven from the herd. It raised its trunk as it caught my scent, and seemed puzzled.

Then the moon rose and showed me up. He saw me, and I saw that his little red eyes glittered in the pale light, which also shone on his huge tusks. All at once the great beast came at me with its trunk curled in the air, as fast as the forest fire and as silent as a snake. With its great ears spread wide it was on me before I had time to spring properly, and I received a shattering blow in the side from the powerful trunk which knocked me into a thorn bush.

I roared with pain, but I had barely time to scramble to my feet when the elephant turned and charged again. This time I managed to claw my way on to his great broad neck, and there I endeavoured to tear him to small pieces.

I had reckoned without the trunk, however, which flicked me off like a mosquito, and I fell to the ground with a thump. Feeling very dazed as I struggled to my feet, I heard the elephant charge on for a little way. Then he stopped and, turning, began to search for me.

I kept quite still, hoping that he would miss me. As the elephant came nearer I noticed something moving in the bushes near me, and the elephant saw it too for he turned off towards it with a rush.

A large black panther leapt out into the clearing, his tail switching his sides.

I knew there must be something wrong with him. Then in the moonlight I saw that his flanks were full of arrows. The two mad beasts stood glaring for a second, and then the elephant, trumpeting shrilly, charged. The panther sprang straight up at his face, but was seized at once in a grip of iron by the elephant's trunk, whirled aloft, and dashed with a sickening thud against a tree. The elephant then knelt on the body, breaking every bone in it, and gored it with his tusks, which showed red in the moonlight.

I did not stay any longer, but slipped noiselessly away. The wind was blowing in my direction, and I knew that he would not scent me.

I quickly regained the path made by the deer, and feeling very stiff and bruised I sat down under the cover of a bush and licked myself all over, pulling out many thorns from my body, after which I felt better and continued to follow my original trail.

After some time I came to a large river where all the tracks disappeared, and I saw that the herds must have crossed here.

I did not feel up to crossing the broad stream, so I turned back along the path by which I had come until I came to another track which crossed the main one. This I followed up, and at last I came upon a sambhur doe sleeping; and creeping round a tree near her I climbed it, and I was able by crawling along an overhanging branch to spring straight on to her back, and I despatched her at once.

I made my meal where I was, and having gorged my fill I reascended the tree, and finding a comfortable crotch about twenty feet from the ground, I watched the glowing eyes of the jackals close in round the remnants of my feast.

SEVEN

SOME weeks passed quite peacefully after my elephant adventure before anything noteworthy happened. I was living in my cave at the time and feeding to a large extent upon the villagers' herds.

They increased their guard, but the men were afraid of me, and most of them ran on seeing me; also, they had no sense of smell, and as they themselves smelt quite strongly I had a great advantage over them.

But they were able on their part to pick up stones and make them fly in rather a puzzling manner, though the worst of all were the arrows which I often broke off short, and the points remained in me and rankled.

At last it appeared that the head man of the village became so angry at losing his cattle that he sent for the white men who lived in a small town twenty miles south. He had asked them to kill a tiger, for none of them had seen me for any length of time. So when the beaters and elephants came upon me in a lot of elephant grass they were evidently surprised to find me so large (as I had been growing very fast and was as large as a very big tiger).

On seeing the elephants I was much alarmed, but seeing there was no possible means of escape I charged the nearest, hoping to take him by surprise.

I sprang high on to his shoulder, and there I saw the little brown man who had tracked me nearly a month ago. He struck at me with an iron rod, but missed, and I knocked him off the elephant's back.

Then I heard a terrific bang, and turning I saw another man in a kind of hut, and in his hands was one of the shiny sticks with which I had been hurt before.

This man was quite white, rather like a dead man, and behind him was another, pointing his stick at me.

I sprang at him. I saw the flash and heard the deafening boom again. Then something hit me on the top of my head, and the world seemed to spin round and I heard the trumpeting of the elephant very faintly, and then I remember nothing more.

When my sense returned I was stretched on the ground, and there was a circle of white men standing around me. One said: "A queer sort of tiger, isn't it?"

"I think it's a sort of overgrown snow-leopard myself," replied the young man who had shot me.

Then I moved and they were much alarmed. "Look out – the thing's only stunned," said one.

"Get those bear nets – take it alive," rejoined another.

I half rose – giddy and sick, but a man behind me brought down the heavy end of a stick on my head, and I lost consciousness again in a world of stars.

When I came round again I was enveloped in yards and yards of stout net tied at the top with a rope. I kicked and bit at the nets, but it was of no use, so I stopped.

Some men approached me with long poles. I struggled to get at them, but they were not in the least alarmed. And coming nearer they thrust the poles under the net, and each man taking hold of one pole-end they carried me roaring and struggling towards the place where the elephants were standing.

This caused me considerable alarm, but the elephants, who actually appeared to be obeying the men, took very little notice of me, except one of the little elephants who was trumpeting.

I was conveyed to a small thing that resembled a box mounted on circular discs which went round, and I afterwards found out it was a cart.

After a while I lay still, and after that I smelt some bullocks, which the men were driving towards me. Soon the cart began to move, to my surprise, for I saw no legs on it. However, the mystery was soon solved, for I twisted round and saw that the bullocks were dragging it along.

We soon came to a village, and hundreds of people came out to look at me. They retired hurriedly when I roared.

Soon they became bolder, and one young man got a long stick and poked me with it, and another threw a stone at me.

Presently, however, one of the white men came out of a hut and drove them away.

Then the journey recommenced, and I was jolted over about ten miles before we came to a halt again.

Night was approaching, and I was beginning to wonder if we would ever stop when one of the men who was leading the bullocks trod on a dust snake and expired on the spot, to my great glee.

The party stopped, and as night was falling they drew up all the carts in a wide circle, in the centre of which the elephants and bullocks were put, evidently for protection against tigers or panthers, which were very abundant in this region.

Over my cart they fastened several logs, so that it was impossible for me to get out. However, I tried till morning, flinging myself against the sides and the logs, and I roared myself hoarse, so that the ten men who were posted by the cart appeared somewhat concerned for their own safety.

Once I cracked a board in the side of the cart and the effect was magical. Men left me in a body, going to the tents and huts which they had erected, and they set up a chattering which would have done credit to the largest band of monkeys.

Finally they came back with more pieces of wood with which they strengthened the sides of the cart.

When they had done this they retired still chattering.

When morning came I was very hot and tired, and when the cart began to move again I felt very bruised and battered, and as we journeyed until midday I was feeling remarkably savage when eventually we stopped in the street of a large village.

Here the party scattered, and I was driven with the elephants to the house of one of the white men, where many people came out to look at me. Soon the men with the poles reappeared, and after untying the logs they got me out. After carrying me past the house they went into a large courtyard, where they dropped me heavily and banged a huge door.

This courtyard was paved with stones and it had walls on every side rising twenty feet. One of the walls was also the side of the house, and had holes in it, at all of which were faces of people looking at me.

I struggled with the nets for quite three-quarters of an hour with no success before I saw the gate open, and the young man whom I had attacked on the back of the elephant came in with a long stick at the end of which was a knife, which he stretched forward and with which after a few moments he managed to cut the ropes, after which he retired hurriedly.

In about five minutes I disentangled myself. After pacing round and round the enclosure I tried to jump the walls, but it was impossible; so after knocking myself about a good deal I stopped, feeling extremely angry.

Soon I saw some men at one of the holes and they were holding a small pig which squealed, which they lowered down with a rope, and it ran round and round my enclosure.

I killed it almost at once, and taking it to a dark corner I consumed it, as I had had no food for two days. After which I snatched a little sleep and then felt calmer.

I was soon awakened by the chattering of some monkeys on the walls, after which night fell and I dozed off.

I did not sleep at all well, however, and I dreamt of elephants and guns in which my mother seemed mixed up.

Just after daybreak a number of children began throwing stones from one of the holes in the wall, and this made me exceedingly angry, and roaring I jumped up at the holes. I had never jumped so high as I did that time, and although I did not actually reach the hole I alarmed them so that they did not appear again.

In about an hour I saw two men with a small pig again, which they lowered, which, however, was tied this time by one leg. I darted at it hoping to snatch it away before it had time to recover.

As soon as I reached it, however, a net fell over me which was drawn rapidly together by a cord from the bottom, and I was trapped again.

EIGHT

THEN the door of the courtyard opened and the brown men with their poles came in. They carried me through into the house along several passages and at length into a great hall down the sides of which many cages with animals were placed, and one of the animals saw me – it was a panther.

He roared and I roared back at him, and then a brown bear joined in, and in a few moments the whole place was in an uproar. But above all I heard the mocking bellow of an alligator.

They carried me to an empty cage and pushed me through the door, untying the net through the bars. I was between a bear on one side and a grey ape on the other, both of which renewed their noise immediately. I was almost too dispirited to answer, but I showed what I thought of them quite plainly.

Soon, however, the noises died down, and retiring to a heap of straw I slept, for I was quite worn out.

On the next morning I awoke with a start, expecting to see the sun as usual coming through the open door of my cave, but there was no light at all in the cold grey room, and I despaired of ever seeing the sun and feeling the cool wind again.

To pass the time I began pacing up and down my cage, up and down with just the same number of steps, and the monotonous regularity of the bars in front of me whichever way I turned appalled me.

My impotence and wretchedness filled me with a mad unreasoning rage, and I tore round and round the cage roaring like a mad beast.

The other occupants of the room were all aroused by the din which I made, and together we created a horrible uproar which, however, soon subsided, and I resumed my pacing up and down.

I noticed that the ape in the cage next to me was climbing up and down a rope and swinging to and fro. I stopped and watched him for a while. First he climbed up the rope, poked his hand out between the bars, and took some straw from a box which was balanced on the top of the cage. Then he came down again and put his handful on a heap which he had already collected. He did this several times until he had gathered enough to make a comfortable bed into which he burrowed, only to come out again in about five minutes and move the whole lot to another corner.

My attention was soon drawn from the ape as a man came in pushing a little cart in front of him, on which were some large pieces of meat.

When the man entered all the animals began to get very excited. They ran up and down and roared and growled. I saw the man take one of the pieces of meat and put it on an iron hook and thrust it into the panther's cage, then he shook it off. Then he passed down the line of cages, feeding all the animals. He began to get nearer to me, and I saw the bear in an absolute frenzy of anticipation. The man opened a little door in my cage and thrust in a piece of meat.

I hurled myself at the bars trying to get at him. The meat was hardly eatable, it smelt strongly of man and had hardly any blood in it.

The man passed on to the ape and gave him some food, then going back to the end of the hall he opened a little door in the back of the panther's cage by pulling a little rope in front. The panther went out at the back.

Having done this to nearly all the cages he came to the bear, who went out as if used to it; and soon his cage was clean. The man passed by me and went out at the end of the room, returning shortly with a little cart with bowls of water. When he gave me mine I hurled myself so violently against the bars that I knocked it into his face, and he hurriedly passed on to the ape.

Later the man brought in a great deal more straw, which he put into the cages. I could not see where the animals went, and most of them seemed to have so little spirit that none of them attempted to escape.

Three days passed and precisely the same thing happened. On the second day I ate my meat, which was not really so bad, but in the meanwhile my cage was becoming almost unbearable. On the third day, however, three of the white men came in and looked at all the animals, and when they came to me I recognised the man who had shot me, and I growled and spat at him through the bars. Then they all made a noise somewhat like that of a hyena just before a meal.

One of them called for the man who fed the animals, and they chatted together for some time, at the end of which he went out and soon returned with a little cart.

Then the young man – whom I shall call my master from now on – came up to my cage and made encouraging noises. But I was suspicious and growled unceasingly.

But he moved about in an even sort of way and didn't jerk about and alarm me. Then he opened the back of the cage and I slipped out and found myself in a pleasant open space about twenty-five feet square, which was completely enclosed by iron bars which prevented escape. It was carpeted by grass and had a large broken tree in the middle. I hadn't seen the sky for some days and I was remarkably pleased to be in the open with the sun shining on me again. Then in the longer grass at the end of the paddock I saw a very large rat, which I killed at once. It was much nicer than the bloodless meat which the men gave me.

Soon I heard a noise behind me and, turning, I saw the door rise. I was determined not to go back to the smelly cage, so I remained where I was. Soon the direction of the wind changed and I noticed a somewhat familiar scent which was that of an elephant. The scent became stronger, and an elephant with a man on its back came walking along the path in front of the open cages.

I thought of my first elephant, and perceiving that discretion was the better part of valour, I darted through the door, which banged behind me. Once in the cage I roared my defiance at elephants and the world in general. Then I remembered that the elephants were tame and obeyed the men, and this must have been a tame one.

I looked round the cage and saw to my relief that it had been cleaned; some fresh water was in my trough and some straw had been thrown into one corner.

In the front of the cage, just between the bars, was a large piece of meat, and I saw that the bear was straining to get his paws through the bars to get my meat. Thinking that if I didn't get it at once I shouldn't get it at all, I took it to the back of the cage. It was very juicy and obviously was fairly fresh. Leaving the bear in a furious rage, with one paw firmly wedged between the bars of his cage, I consumed it slowly.

After eating half of the meat I washed and regained my sleek appearance. Then I lay curled up in the straw till night came, when I was awakened by the sound of footsteps.

I jumped up and saw my master approaching from the entrance; he was carrying a basket in his hands, and I thought that I smelt some animal.

He walked straight down the rows of cages until he came opposite to me, when he stopped and began to advance slowly. I growled.

He advanced to the front of the cage, making soothing noises. I retreated as far as possible feeling very apprehensive, and for a few moments he continued his silly noises. Then he took from the basket the carcase of a jack rabbit and threw it to me.

The sudden movement which he made in throwing it made me start; however, he made no other movement, and I think if I had not just had a large meal I would have taken it, but as it was I left it lying and snarled and spat at him.

Soon he left to my great relief, for my nerves were all on edge. After he had gone I ate the rabbit, which was very nice and did not smell of man as much as the ordinary food.

Then having licked myself all over very thoroughly, I paced up and down my cage for the best part of an hour. Then I lay down in the straw and slept for a while, only to be awakened by a sharp pain in the tail.

Jumping up, I saw that the ape had seized my tail and was pulling it. I jerked it away with a roar.

I mention this as an example of things which I had to put up with.

At length night fell and I slept well.

NINE

FOR many weeks my master continued to clean out my cage and feed me, and gradually I got so used to his presence that I even forgot to growl at him. But when anyone else came, such as the native who cleaned the other cages, an ungovernable rage seized me and I hurled myself against the bars until I was sore.

One day my master stayed away, and then I realised how unpleasant it was to be without him to clean out my cage or feed me, for no one else would come near me. Next day, however, he returned and I had fresh straw and a clean cage; but when he was cleaning the cage and I was in the paddock I accidentally trod on a thorn which, with a small branch attached, had blown from a tree near by. With a snarl I broke off the branch and thought no more of it until the next morning, when my foot was painful and it made me limp.

But by midday the paw had become twice its proper size, and it throbbed very painfully. My master seemed to notice it, but he did nothing, as I was so angry that I would have killed him if he had entered my cage. By evening I felt so unwell that I did not even retaliate when the ape pulled my tail, who soon left me alone, or when the bear, nearly tearing himself in two with the effort, took the meat which I hadn't touched, having no appetite. I got very little sleep that night and I felt as if I did not mind what happened to me.

Next day my master did not come until the evening, when he stood outside my cage for some time making his usual silly noises. Then very slowly he opened the cage door and came in.

I growled and half rose, but he showed no signs of fear and continued to approach. Then bending he lifted my paw. I growled, but I did not snatch it away as I hardly had strength to do so.

With a quick tug he pulled out the thorn – and I snarled at the pain, but I had the sense to see that he was trying to help me. Then he squeezed the paw gently and a lot of matter came out which at once relieved the pain. He tied a piece of cloth round it, and backed out of the cage, shutting the door.

Soon after that I dozed off into a refreshing sleep. I slept well all night, and next morning I woke up feeling much better and also extremely hungry. I could move about quite well, and after a time I worried the bandage so much that it came off, and I licked my paw, until I saw the native attendant coming in with his little cart, and I so far recovered my spirits as to roar lustily at him. Then I lay down in a corner of my cage where the sun could shine in and idly watched the ape swinging on his rope.

After about an hour I began to doze, but I was awakened by the sound of my master's voice, who was standing outside the cage with the basket which he always carried when he came to me. I was pleased to see him, partly because I knew that his coming meant a good meal and partly because I had some feelings of gratitude towards him.

He smiled and pulled the rope that opened the door at the back of the cage. I went out and heard him enter. Soon he had finished and I came in again, expecting to find my piece of meat. But there was not a vestige of food in the cage. I went to the front of the cage and there he stood outside with a piece of meat in his hand. He cut a piece off, and I wondered whether he were going to eat it.

He did not eat it, however, on the contrary he threw it through the bars at me. It landed at my feet. I sniffed it suspiciously, and then finding it all right I snapped it up. Then he threw another piece, this time a little nearer to himself, then another and another, until at last I was almost feeding from his hand.

Curiously enough I felt no alarm. There was one more piece, and this he held just between the bars and did not throw it. I wondered if he would suddenly hit me if I took it. Then I saw what a juicy piece it was and my hunger overcame my fear. With a quick snap I took it out of his hand and jumped back to the end of the cage.

To my surprise he showed no signs of anger, merely smiled, and withdrawing his hand went away.

I paced up and down for some time, thinking how curious it was that I should take my food from the hand of a man, and that I could have cracked that man's skull like a bird's egg, and that I should permit him to enter my cage to extract a thorn.

The idea, however, did not anger me as it would have done a month ago. I merely thought it to be curious and dismissed it from my mind, and started to wash. I had little else to do.

Later in the day a diversion occurred in the form of a small grey monkey who had come in from one of the paddocks when the cages were being cleaned.

He had remained in the cage of a very old panther, who did not find him for some time. The monkey squeezed through the bars at the top of the cage and raced up and down the top of the other cages, until he came to the tank where a huge tame alligator was kept, almost opposite to me, where he missed his footing and fell. The alligator, who had been as still as a log all day, suddenly reared out of the water and caught the unfortunate monkey in mid-air.

It took several minutes for the pandemonium to die down again. Later on in the day I caught a large rat which was amongst my straw.

TEN

SIX uneventful months passed, during which my master and I got to know each other very well. I for my part understood that he did not mean to hit me nor shoot me, and he was always very kind and fed me and cleaned my cage.

One day he came into my cage as usual and opened the door at the back. I went out, but instead of hearing the door close I turned round and saw to my surprise that he had followed me. In his hand was a large ball. "Here, Cæsar," he said (he always called me Cæsar). Thinking for a moment that it was alive, I pounced on it and caught it in my teeth. He seemed pleased, but when I began to worry it he made a noise and patted his knee.

He seemed to want something, but I could not quite understand what he meant, though I saw dimly that it was to do with the ball. He bent down and flicked his fingers, then in a flash I understood that he wanted the ball. Picking it up I took it to him and put it at his feet. He seemed pleased, and scratched me behind the ears, which I liked.

He took the ball again and rolled it to one corner of the enclosure, saying at the time, "Fetch it, Cæsar."

Seeing that he wanted me to get it again, I went and fetched it, but I thought that he was rather foolish to throw it away if he really wanted to keep it. Then after we had done this for ten times he observed that I was getting tired of it, and he went in to clean the cage while I lay in the sun pretending to be asleep, but really watching a large lizard creeping along in the grass. Its beady little black eyes were taking in everything. As soon as it came near enough I suddenly shot out my paw, but of course I was not nearly quick enough, and almost too quickly for my eye to follow, the lizard had darted across the enclosure and out between the bars, leaving only a little dust and its tail behind it.

I went back into the cage and saw that my master was tying the ball so that it was suspended about three feet from the floor. After he had gone I happened to bang against it, and seeing it swing as if it were alive, I turned to look at it and it hit me on the nose. I struck at it but it swung just out of my reach. I kept on patting it for some time, then I went to sleep for a while, but some mosquitoes woke me up. Feeling bored I patted at the ball again, just to see it swing, and back it came, and I pretended it was a living animal and growled at it.

On the back swing it seemed to be running away and I patted it again, this time from the side, and it went round on a circular course, like a bird; in fact, I was having quite a game with it when my master came back with my food and water, which was rather late. He also had a specially tasty little piece of meat, which I took from his hand as usual. Nearly every day for some months he had brought me some special thing, and on every seventh day a pig – a whole pig.

I started playing with the ball again, and I was amazed to find how fat and out of condition I was. In fact, after about half an hour's exercise I was quite tired and perspiring freely. However, it did me good, for I slept better that night than on any other occasion.

Next morning I was a little stiff, but with a fine appetite. Soon my master came and we went out into the paddock together. He had another ball, which he threw to me as before. In a short time we were having quite a game with it. He pretended to throw it one way and threw it another. I pretended to be very angry and growled. In the end I unfortunately bit the ball in two. So he went in to clean my cage.

While he was doing this a small bird settled on the ground near me, and I tried to catch it but I was too slow. Then I saw how fat I was really getting, and I decided to exercise my body more by means of the ball. So when I got into my cage about half an hour later I knocked the ball about quite energetically, and by midday I had invented a game. I stood on the side of a crack in the stone floor of my cage and the ball hung just over it, and if on the back swing it got past me, it had escaped – if not, I had caught it.

During the next three weeks I learned how to bring the ball when I was told. We had long games with the ball sometimes, and I became very adept at catching it. As the days wore on I began to look forward to the time when he came to feed me, and I was quite anxious if he was late; and I also became so used to my cage and ready-killed food that I hardly believed that I was the same panda, who could pull down a water buffalo and think nothing of it. I do not believe that if at the time I had been set free I could have supported myself comfortably.

One day when I was in my paddock, as the door had been left open all day, the air suddenly became colder and the sky dark, and I had a horrible feeling that something terrible was going to happen. The other animals who were also in their paddocks (as their cages were being cleaned) seemed very frightened. The bear next to me started running round and round uttering a curious whimpering noise, and on the other side the ape was leaping about and chattering as if demented. Everything was as still as death, not a breeze enough to move the aspen trees on the path outside, and not a sound other than that of the animals. Then all at once the sun seemed to go out like a dead firefly and a chill that sent a shiver down my back came with its going. Now all the animals were quiet and not even a gnat buzzed, and in the distance I heard a dog howling. One would have thought that the world was dead.

In a few minutes my master came out, and after looking up to the sky for a few moments he came over to me and put his hand over my eyes and stroked me. I was badly frightened and trembling, so I snuggled my head under his arms, and he said in an even voice: "Keep calm, old boy – it's only an eclipse."

I did not know what he meant, but anyhow it was very soothing. In a few minutes after that the sun seemed to light up again.

ELEVEN

SO FAR I have only mentioned the pleasant side of my life in captivity, but there was quite another side. Can you imagine the utter dreariness of the long hours between the times when my master came and fed me and the night? If so, you will be able to understand my intense hatred for all men, except my master and a few others.

Men had taken me from my home, from the jungle with its infinite variety of life and colour, and had put me in a cage with bars and a cold stone floor. A paddock or small plot of withered grass was my jungle and the barred cage was my lair.

For a flowing stream to drink from I had a small stone trough, and instead of the pleasure of tracking, stalking and then killing my prey, I was given at a regular time every day a smelly, stale and bony lump of flesh with no blood in it.

That which I missed most of all was the killing of my own food. It is true that I was always given enough. But what could compensate for the thrill of the charge, and then the last wild gallop before I reached its neck and it fell dead? What could rival the warm blood and juicy meat of which I was particularly fond?

However, on the whole I was not too unhappy, and the ball which had been hung up was a great consolation, and in a few weeks I knew every curl that it would make.

My dislike of the brown man who cleaned the other cages grew in intensity as time wore on.

One day after my master had fed me and cleaned my cage this little hyena of a man came with a long slender stick of bamboo and tormented me with it. In vain I tried to catch it and crush it to pieces, for I could not move with any rapidity in the tiny space I had, and he lashed me again and again with it, laughing all the time. I hated that mocking laugh, which was as if a hyena had got into a man's body.

At another time he snatched my pig from my cage, having driven me into a corner with a spiked iron rod. As I have said, my master brought me a pig every seven days, and I looked forward to this as they were always very fresh and tender. Besides, I had always been very partial to pig.

At another time he purposely upset my water, so that it ran out of the cage. He always did these things after my master had gone, so as not to be found out. I was always hoping that my master would come back and catch him.

As the months drew into a year I became very attached to my master, who seemed to understand me and I him. He also seemed to know how I felt and behaved accordingly. For instance, if I was feeling poorly he would sit down and stroke me quietly behind the ears and talk to me; or if I was full of spirits we sometimes pretended to fight. It began by my refusing to give up the ball with which we often played, and then he pretended to be very angry and rolled me over on my back; and I roared and snarled as if I would eat him, while he rolled me over and over as if I was a little cub. As for hurting him, I would have perished before doing so.

He taught me to obey him and, among other things, to carry and fetch, and to even leave my food when he told me. I could not understand why he made me do this, but there was a reason.

One day he brought into my cage a steel chain and a collar of thick leather. The leather collar had a leather buckle which fixed it to the chain. He opened it and calling me to him fastened it round my neck, and we went out into the paddock where he fastened the chain to it.

At first I disliked it, but within two weeks I had become quite accustomed to it. He also trained me to stay still and not move until he called me.

One day when he had finished the cleaning of my cage he fastened the chain on as usual, but instead of going out into the paddock, to my great surprise he opened the cage door and led me out. At first I did not like to come, but when he said "Come on, Cæsar," and tugged the chain, I jumped down to the floor by his side.

How curious it was to feel different ground under one's feet, for in one year I had grown to know every stone in the floor in my cage and almost every blade of grass in the paddock.

My master led me down the passage between the cages, and out at the entrance and through two rooms, and out into a large enclosure in which there was a large stretch of green, very short-cropped grass. The walls of this paddock were made of brick, and they were about ten feet high. At the foot of each of these walls there was a space in which the earth had been turned up and flowers were growing in orderly rows.

I wondered how they got there, and I came to the conclusion that the ants must have put them there, for the ants are very fond of going about together in lines. Also I had seen when turning over an ant-hill in search of a rat that the ants had several of the small things from which the plants grow stored up.

I did not have much time to wonder, however, before my master said, "Here, Cæsar – meet my wife," and turning I saw a female who evidently was my master's mate. I growled at her.

But he stopped me and said, "Down, old boy."

The female was without fear, and put her hand on my head, and at once I felt that she was friendly towards me. My master said, "This is your mistress, Cæsar," so hereafter I shall call her my mistress. Then my master took the chain from my collar and the ball from his pocket, with which we had a fine game in which they threw it from one to the other and I tried to catch it.

After we had finished my mistress sat down and made a great fuss of me. I saw that my master was pleased so I permitted her to stroke me to her heart's content. Besides, it saved me the trouble of a wash. Soon he put the chain on me again and we went back to the cage.

After he had gone the native whom I hated came with his bamboo rod. Inserting this through the bars he suddenly hit me on the nose. The blow stung and I roared. This is what he wanted, and, laughing, he struck at me again.

Leaping to the back of the cage I observed that my master had left his hat on the floor. The man had not seen this, however, and continued to torment me, while I hoped against hope that my master would come back for it.

Soon I saw the door open as he entered and, roaring, I hurled myself against the bars to attract his attention. Just then the wretched man gave me a particularly vicious crack.

In a few strides he reached the man, and seizing him by the shoulder, he said in a quiet tone: "What is the meaning of this?"

The man said something which I did not catch. My master with great speed drew back his fist and dealt the man a blow on the jaw, knocking him off his feet into a corner. I thought that my master would now kill him, but he let the man lie. Then he came into my cage, and after giving me the cane, which I tore to fragments, and stroking me, he took his hat and left.

Soon after this two natives came and took my tormentor away, who was almost stupefied but had just enough energy to shake his fist at me as he was taken away.

Next day another native cleaned the cages out, but he kept clear of me, to my very great content.

TWELVE

A FEW days later my master took me into the garden again, where I saw his two young children, which were quite like him, only very small. They smelt the same. I was very proud that he should trust me so much and determined not to hurt them, for evidently he liked them, though they would have made a tender and juicy meal.

My mistress stood guard over them and appeared very anxious, very like my mother was over me. They were not in the least afraid of me, to my surprise, and made rather pleasant gurgling noises.

Then my master took one of them in his arms and held it quite near to my face, and it chuckled, putting one of its podgy hands on my head, and I realised that these were quite pleasant little creatures. Very soon, however, they were removed and my master and I went through the garden gate. We emerged on an open courtyard in which there were several stables in the walls, all of which were empty except one, and from this I caught the scent of some animal that I did not know.

Then my master attached the end of my chain to a ring in the wall, and said very slowly and impressively: "Stay there, Cæsar"; and I knew from long weeks of training what he meant.

He had taught me to obey him absolutely, and I would have as soon thought of flying as of disobeying. Then he went to the occupied stable and led out a great beast like a buffalo, but taller and less thick. Its tail was composed of long hairs and its head was bent at right angles to the neck and it had no horns. This extraordinary animal was evidently tame.

On seeing me it reared up and made a loud noise, and I growled, but my master said: "Be quiet, Cæsar." The animal would not be calmed, so he got it back with difficulty to the stables. Then he came to me, and after he had unfastened the chain, he said:

"Well, Cæsar, and what do you think of my horse?"

I did not understand what he said, but afterwards he said "horse" a great many times, so I concluded that the creature was called a horse, and I wondered what it was for.

When we reached the cage I went in as usual after he had removed the chain, and he remained a little while outside talking to me. I did not understand what he said, but I liked the sound of his voice. The word horse kept re-occurring, and I thought he was trying to make me understand something about it. Although I went over all my ideas of his words I could not get his meaning. Soon he went away and left me to puzzle over this animal.

Before nightfall I came to these conclusions:

First, the beast was tame;

Second, my master had shown signs of liking it;

Third, he had stopped me from hurting it by chaining me up.

On the following morning after cleaning the cage he took me to the courtyard, and after fastening my chain to the ring in the wall he brought out the horse, and after a while he took it back again, and then we went back to my cage. This happened on the next day and on the one after that, and so on until I lost count.

At the end of all this time the horse and I got quite used to each other, and at last I comprehended that my master wanted me to like the horse, and he also wanted the horse not to be afraid of me. Then after a month had passed the horse didn't fear me any longer, and I no longer wanted to kill and eat it.

Then one day my master brought out a kind of seat made to fit the horse's back, and after strapping this on he brought from the stable a piece of metal and some leather thongs. The piece of metal he passed under the horse's tongue, and the horse, who seemed quite used to it, stood still. Then to my amazement he jumped on the horse's back, which by means of the leather straps was entirely under his control. Then they went out of the gate, and he said to me:

"Stay there, Cæsar."

Soon he returned, and after he had put the horse back we went back to my cage.

One day in the next week we went out through the garden to the horse's stable, and when my master had put on the harness as he called it, he took a longer chain and fastened it to my original one; then he mounted the horse, and taking my chain in his hand he rode out of the gate and I followed. At first the horse was very excited and tried to get away from me, but he soon calmed down, as my master spoke to him soothingly. We emerged on to a grassy plain, extending in short bushy folds as far as the eye could see.

How good it was to have the crisp grass under my feet and to see an uninterrupted horizon all round. As we went I reflected on the remarkable conditions under which I was existing, and observed to myself how strange it was that anyone like myself should be found fastened by a chain to an animal of which he should be making a good meal, and obeying every word of a man seated on the back of this horse.

My reverie, however, was cut short by a hole in the ground, in which I half tripped. My master laughed, and saying "Come on, old boy – keep up," made the horse gallop, and we tore along at top speed for a while, which was very pleasant because for a whole year I had not really exerted myself. Having covered three-quarters of a mile we stopped, and I looked at the horse with new respect for it did not appear in the least fatigued, whilst I was panting and sweating a little.

Meanwhile my master had climbed a tree, very clumsily I thought, and was looking round and round as if searching for something, and he came down looking as if he had not found it. Just then the wind changed a little, and I smelt game. My master must have seen it, for he looked pleased and pointed in its direction.

Then an antelope came into sight, feeding on the short grass, and my master crouched down at once so as not to be seen. Then he unfastened my chain and said to me: "Fetch it, Cæsar." I understood what he meant and determined to show him what I could do. I was off in a moment, wriggling through the bushes in my most skilful fashion. At first I was so clumsy that I was afraid the creature would see me, but soon all my old cunning returned and I got within killing range.

The antelope saw me and I charged. Though the beast was very fleet, and I had to exert myself to my utmost speed, I soon secured him. Having broken its neck, I began to lap up the warm blood; but in a few moments I was checked by hearing my master's voice calling: "Leave it, Cæsar."

THIRTEEN

LOOKING up I saw him standing about twenty yards away, looking at me steadily.

I thought: "Why should I give up my kill to this man?" Then a remembrance of all his past kindness made me hesitate to disobey; but a smell of warm blood was wafted up from the antelope and almost killed my better feeling.

Then the habit of implicit obedience which I had formed came uppermost, and I picked up the animal and going to him laid it at his feet. He did not do much; he just said "Good, Cæsar," and patted me on the head, but I felt amply repaid for my sacrifice.

After this he picked up the antelope and went back to the horse which had been tied to a tree. Having slung it on to the horse's back, he mounted, and we went back to the house. When he had put the horse back into its stable we went back to my cage, and my master gave me a large piece of the antelope's shoulder, and I remembered that I always used to begin my meal at the shoulder of my prey instead of at the haunch, as I had seen some animals doing.

After I had eaten every scrap I paced up and down my cage pondering over the curious chain of events which had made up my life so far, and I wondered why I did not escape when I had the chance. In a way I was glad that I had not, but on the other hand I thought how pleasant it would be if I were back again in my old cave where I was born and going wherever I wished and feeding at my own time. But on reflection I thought it would be even better if my master were with me.

My thoughts occupied me until nightfall, when my tail was suddenly seized by the ape, who had thrust his hand through the bars of both his cage and mine and got a grip on my tail when I turned during my walking up and down. I tried to jerk it away, but the ape had a firm hold, so I whisked round and before he could withdraw, my teeth had sunk to the bone in his arm.

Pandemonium ensued, and the ape raced round and round his cage chattering and shrieking. After about ten minutes he burrowed into a large box of straw at the back of his cage, from which he did not emerge for a whole day, but gave out dismal howls and moans which interrupted my sleep somewhat.

In a few days' time he was moved up the row away from me, and a cage with a little mongoose, who took no notice of me, was put in his place.

In about a week's time my master took me out again. This time, however, we met a native who fled towards the village. I set off after him with a roar, but the combined strength of my master and the horse pulled me up. My master appeared very angry, and I sulked for a short while, but I soon recovered my spirits, observing to myself that one man did not matter, and anyway he would not have tasted nice. I suppose my master felt bound to protect his own kind, but at the time it seemed rather unreasonable to me.

We went on and on, past the place where I killed the antelope and about ten miles south-east until we came to a place which my master and the horse seemed to know. Here we stopped, and as we were all a little fatigued we had a short rest.

Then my master took the horse to a small hut which was hidden among some trees and shut him in. I suppose this was as a protection against wild animals; then he led me by my chain and we went down to a small pool, where I saw some fairly fresh pig-marks. Here my master looked round for some time and at last found some of the more obvious tracks, and I wished that I could have communicated with him in some way to make him understand the bent pieces of grass, a little splash of mud on a stone and, above all, the faint smell of pig in the air, so that he could translate all the signs that pointed to the fact that pigs had been there a little while ago.

But it was no good. All my growls and scratchings he mistook for signs of pleasure, so soon I gave it up.

When he had found several footprints my master took me to them and, selecting a very large one, said: "Fetch him, Cæsar!" I felt a slight sinking of the heart as I saw that it was that of a remarkably large boar, probably the chief of the sounder. But nevertheless I followed the trail along a stretch of very difficult country, all stony with only a sprinkling of grass here and there.

My master followed, still holding the chain, but soon he took it off. He made such a noise in walking and he smelt so strongly that I was afraid we would never get near enough to catch any of them.

However, things turned out better than I had hoped, for after not more than ten minutes of stony ground we reached a lot of long green grass which held the scent, and I could see that the grass had been crushed in places.

Now I went very slowly, for as the scent was very fresh here I felt that we might come on them suddenly. We crept on through the grass, my master crawling with his hands like a rational beast, and we soon found the pigs in a grove of bamboo, eating the tender shoots.

The great boar was feeding with the rest, and as the sentinel pig had not seen us, I hoped to be able to dash in and kill the boar in the confusion.

Then my master sneezed, and in an instant the fat sows and the tender sucking pigs were in full flight. Only the boar stayed to block my path, to let the others escape. He did not think that I was after him, for who would prefer a tough boar to a fat and tender sow?

However, I charged in directly and got my shoulder laid open for my folly, and remembering the tiger whom I had seen killed before, I contented myself with circling round and looking for an opening. I rather wished that my master had had better eyes when he picked out this pig's footprints, but for all that it promised to be a grand fight.

Suddenly I saw an opening as the boar had turned a little too slowly, and I darted in, rolling him over and tearing his flank in my endeavour to pin him down. But in a flash he had whipped round his head and with his tusk had cut into the pad of my right forepaw. Then as I released my hold he rolled over and got on his feet again, aiming a wicked thrust at my unprotected stomach.

With a roar I sprang out of range, and as he was carried on a little way by the impetuosity of his thrust, I leaped in and gave him a blow which smashed his skull in, and he fell kicking feebly. But he was dead almost as soon as he touched the ground.

I am glad that I was able to finish him when I did, for as I was lamed by the cut in my paw I could not have lasted very much longer.

As soon as the boar fell my master came from his hiding-place and walked towards the boar, saying, "Leave it, Cæsar – good boy."

This time I did not hesitate, and left it at once, and went over to him, looking up for approval.

On seeing my blood he knelt down on the grass and took up my injured paw, talking kindly all the time. The place was bleeding fast and hurting abominably, so he tore a large piece from his clothes and wrapped it round the wound. I tried to walk on the paw, but the pain made me desist. Meanwhile my master was covering the hog with a heap of stones. Evidently he did not mean to carry it with him.

Then he set off towards the hut where we had left the horse, and I walked slowly on three legs, and he tried to help me along, but the march back to the hut was the slowest and most painful that I have ever made.

At last we reached it, just after the sun had set.

A panther was prowling around, attracted no doubt by the scent of the horse, which I could hear snorting angrily. The panther cleared off, however, at our approach. The horse, being down-wind of us, caught our scent, and I heard him whinnying with pleasure.

On reaching the hut my master went in, and after searching round for a little while, he brought out a metal box, from which he took a blue bottle containing some brown fluid, which he poured on to my wound.

It stung horribly. At first I thought that he was playing a trick on me, but the thought was foolish, so I dismissed it from my mind at once. Having done this he bound it up again and re-entered the hut and brought out the chain, with which he tied me up to a post, and then he went back to the hut saying, "On guard, Cæsar."

FOURTEEN

I UNDERSTOOD what he meant and I prepared to have a sleepless night. I felt sure that he would not have said "on guard" if he had known how tired I was, and all night I paced up and down, and sometimes lay down, but I never went to sleep, in case a panther, or perhaps a leopard, should come along.

Once or twice I heard the coughing roar of a panther, and again I caught the scent of a leopard, but neither of the creatures attacked me, for which I was extremely thankful, as I could not have held my own against either of them with my paw in the state that it was.

But at last morning came, with one of the most beautiful sunrises that I have ever seen.

Then presently my master woke up, and after harnessing the horse, he set off towards the place where we had left the boar. After taking my chain off, and telling me to have a good sleep, he shut me in the hut.

I heard the noise of the horse die away in the distance and then I went to sleep. Hardly had I closed my eyes, however, when I was awakened by a soft hiss, and starting up I saw a large sized python surveying me with glittering eyes.

I jumped up, and either my eyes were deceiving me or something, for between me and the terrible snake I clearly saw my mother. She looked pale and smoky, but perhaps that was the sleep in my eyes, and I thought I saw her baring her teeth in a snarl at the snake.

The snake glided out of the door, which was slightly ajar.

Then the thought that perhaps she had lived through the fire flashed through my mind, and I started forward with a purr of delight to meet her, but to my horror and amazement there was nothing there. I had gone right through her.

Turning round – I thought perhaps she was hiding, but after searching the hut I was convinced that I must have imagined the whole thing, in a sort of waking dream. But there were still the snake marks in the dust on the floor to explain away, but not the faintest scent of her or a footmark except my own was in the hut.

Greatly puzzled by this incident, I walked up and down trying to solve the mystery, but then almost at once my master came in, with the body of the boar, which he had fetched with the horse.

I suppose he put down my agitation to my wound.

As the cut was practically closed, we set off for the house, and going rather slowly we reached it by midday.

When I was going to my cage I trod on a sharp flint, which opened the cut again, so feeling rather angry and upset I let my master bind it up again, but I soon worried the bandage off as I was feeling rather peevish.

Until nightfall I wondered how to explain the fact that the snake had not appeared at all alarmed at my mother's presence.

All my explanations to myself that it was a dream were swept away by the fact that the snake marks were so obvious that there was no mistaking them.

As I was unable to come to any satisfactory conclusion, I dismissed the matter entirely from my mind and went to sleep.

Early next morning I was awakened by my master calling to me from outside the cage, and he was carrying what seemed like the shoulder of the boar, which he gave to me. After I had consumed it he came into the cage and inspected my paw, which was healing nicely.

After this I went out into the paddock while he cleaned my cage. My master did not take me out again for nearly two weeks, during which time my paw had quite healed and I was feeling very fit.

Then one day a lot of white men came and looked at me. My master was with them, and he brought one old white man into my cage. I was feeling very happy and good-humoured, so after the stranger had got over his first fears I permitted him to stroke my head, very nervously, with the tips of his fingers, standing as far off as possible, while my master was encouraging him. I looked round and caught my master's eye. He smiled and nodded and our amusement was mutual.

Soon the little man became rather boring, and as I wanted to play with my master, I decided to get rid of him, so suddenly springing up I gave a frightful snarl, showing all my teeth, and he left quite hurriedly.

After he had gone my master burst into a roar of laughter, and after producing the chain, we went to the garden, where he told me to stay while he harnessed the horse.

I had just jumped up into the lower branches of a tree which was in the corner of the garden, so as to be in the shade, when I heard the voice of our visitor raised in a somewhat agitated manner. Evidently he was walking down the gravel path outside which led to the garden gate.

Then I heard it open, and into the garden walked my mistress and the old man, who was saying, "I tell you the beast is not safe. It will be escaping some day and eating somebody."

Then I jumped down from the tree to meet my mistress, who always made a fuss of me. The old man let out a bellow like a bull buffalo in pain and disappeared with remarkable speed, leaving a cloud of dust.

My mistress appeared a little flustered at first by her guest's curious behaviour, but just then my master reappeared, and they talked together, and then they both laughed, and my master and I went to the horse, which was getting impatient, and then we went out on to the plain.

This time, however, luck seemed to have deserted us, for in a whole day we sighted only one antelope, and I bungled the stalking of it so badly that it was able to get down-wind of me, and it was off at once.

I thought that I could run it down and set off after it, but I failed dismally, and after I had gone nearly a mile at top speed, and in the end had lost it, I turned and went back to my master, who consoled me with a large piece of the meat which he was eating from a bag.

It had an extraordinary taste, rather interesting, but like no animal that I had ever killed, and there was no blood in it at all. I afterwards found out that men have a curious way of putting their meat over a fire and destroying its delightful original flavour by many quaint devices. Why they did this I could never discover.

Then after the midday siesta we searched for game and followed up many trails but with no success. At last we heard a frightful noise coming from behind a small hill about half a mile distant.

We reached it in a few minutes. Meanwhile the extraordinary noises increased in volume. They mystified and frightened me, and I was wondering what strange beast this might be which howled so horribly, when suddenly we came upon a white man squatting in front of a box which gave out these terrible roars and whines. The beast was evidently imprisoned within it.

The man was not in the least disconcerted by our sudden appearance and continued to belch out smoke from his mouth at intervals. Then he said to my master in a curious kind of voice: "Say Bo – taking the cat out for a run?"

My master laughed and they talked for a little while.

Then he tethered the horse, and together they went over to a kind of cart which was standing about twenty feet away.

Up to this time I had been so utterly petrified with amazement that I had stood perfectly still by the horse, but then the animal in the box gave a particularly violent and high-pitched howl which hurt my ears, so I roared at it to silence it.

My master laughed and then said to the man: "I'm afraid Cæsar has no ear for radio music."

Then the stranger came over to the box and either killed the beast within it or something.

Then my master and the stranger began to do something to the cart. At first I thought that the man had lost the bullock for his cart, but when it suddenly gave out a menacing roar I altered my opinion and roared back at it, thoroughly frightening the horse, who plunged and kicked till my master came over and calmed him.

Soon after this we left the man to his roaring and howling companion and went homeward. Before we had got far, however, I heard the cart give a violent roar which I answered, but it easily outroared me, and it never seemed to pause for breath. When I began another roar my master stopped me by saying, "Perhaps motor-cars don't agree with you, Cæsar – but you needn't tell the whole world about it."

FIFTEEN

FOR the next months we did a lot of hunting with various success, mostly the smaller antelopes, who sometimes came quite near the house.

Once I killed a small Nilgai or blue bull, after a struggle in which I got rather nastily gored, but my master intervened and shot the creature with his revolver.

During this time I saw quite a lot of his children. They grew rapidly, and I liked them almost as if they were my own cubs. But one day I missed them, all except the smallest, and then I remembered having seen them start on a journey.

My master seemed rather silent and sad after they had gone, and when my mistress and the youngest went a week after he became quite melancholy, and spent most of his time with the horse and with me, sometimes going great distances up to the mountains, where I caught some fine ibex and bharals and we saw some red pandas.

My master always appeared very surprised at the way I could follow even the fastest in this very rocky and dangerous country, but I thought it was scarcely surprising. Most of my food during my life had been derived from mountain goats and wild sheep, so that I was adept at hunting them.

Speaking of red pandas, I have seen many more of them than of my own type, which is so much larger than they are.

Besides, who would have a silly red coat instead of a clean white one, with such fine black ears?

My indignation was great when my master caught and tried to tame a nasty smelly red panda, spending quite a lot of time with it instead of with me.

However, one day it poked its head through the bars and made foolish noises at me, trying to make friends, no doubt. But, to punish its impudence, I bit its head right off, and so stopped its idiotic chauntering.

My master was very angry and took no notice of me for three days, but I had the satisfaction of knowing that he could no longer like the red panda.

As I have said, my mother was a very large snow-leopard, and this accounts for the fact that I was growing so very large. Also, my legs, unlike those of most great pandas, were growing quite long, and I could run very fast.

About this time the spring was coming on and my summer coat was growing. I noticed a lot of blackish spots on my new fur which I thought greatly enhanced my appearance.

A week after I killed the red panda my master took me out hunting again. This time we went on for four days right up to the foothills of the great range of mountains, which I had seen from my cave and which was about eighty miles to the west.

After we had stayed there for two days, hunting sha and bharal, we ascended half-way up the nearest of the mountains. It was hardly a mountain, but really only a large foothill, being the top of a long ridge, which extended right and left, before we came to the real heights. We left the horse tethered near the tent in which my master always slept.

On reaching that part of the mountain where the snow always lay I killed an ibex, which my master skinned and cut up, putting the very best pieces into his knapsack and giving me the rest. Then we went still higher up, and I noticed my master was breathing with difficulty. So we stopped, and after looking all round at the vast extent of land below us, we began to descend. I stayed behind, finishing the last pieces of the ibex, and after a few minutes my master turned and called me.

He did not appear to be able to see me until I moved, and for the first time I saw the use of my white coat, which made me quite invisible against the snow. After about two hours we reached the horse, which was feeding on some of the scanty grass which was the vegetation. He was pleased to see us, and, as he had broken his rope, he trotted up to my master, who patted his neck, and I felt rather jealous but did not show it.

When night fell my master made a fire and cooked the pieces of ibex in a pot full of melted snow.

Then next morning he put the tent down and we all ascended the mountain side. The horse was a lot of trouble, but at last we got about half-way up. He put the tent up again behind a huge boulder where there was no snow. It was hard for him to fix the tent pegs, but at last he found a patch of ground with a little grass on it.

Soon he had a fire on the bare rock, where he cooked some more of the ibex, some of which he gave to me.

Later in the day he shot a goat (which I had missed) which had darted up a pinnacle of rock. This was the most remarkable piece of rock which I had ever seen, jutting straight out into the air over a precipice of about two thousand feet. The goat, on being shot, bounded into the air and luckily fell our side of the precipice.

As the cold was intense my master made a coat from the skin of this goat and the ibex, which he wore with the fur inside. At the time I remember I thought human skin must be very poor protection against the cold.

On the next day, as I was following a very large goat up a sharp incline towards the peak, it suddenly disappeared from view behind a rock. In a few minutes I had reached the place, but the goat was nowhere to be seen. Then I observed a narrow fissure in the mountain side through which it must have gone. I thought I had him now for certain, as in his terror he had fled into a blind alley.

This was not so, however, for on investigation the fissure proved to lead into a roughly circular tunnel, down which I could dimly see the goat.

Its hoof-beats echoed and re-echoed till it sounded like twenty goats. I followed it for some way, but it seemed to know the twists and turns of the tunnel, and after turning a corner, before I had time to see where I was going, it darted off into a side turning leading off the main one.

I ran on for some little way and passed several tunnels which led off the one I was following. I think I passed five before I came to a place where the main passage split into four. Rapidly selecting one, I darted down it and charged full tilt into a very chilly and deep stream. Scrambling out I pursued my course until I realised that the goat must have escaped me.

I began to retrace my steps, and after crossing the stream I came to the place where the tunnels converged, and I wondered which one I had come by. I chose one, of course the wrong one, but I followed it until I saw a glint of light at the end.

Soon I emerged, but instead of finding myself on the familiar ground about half a mile from the tent, I was standing on the top of a pleasant grassy slope going down with a gentle incline to a small lake, fed by the stream into which I had fallen, which gurgled out into a little waterfall to my left.

About ten miles across this valley the real mountains extended in a vast unbroken line as far as I could see.

Then I understood that I must have gone right through the mountain, which was no doubt honeycombed by these tunnels. The idea came to me that if I could get back I could lead my master through by this way and save him the painful and slow ascent of the mountain, as he obviously intended to get over to this side.

So, turning, I went back by the path I had come, and I noticed that all the way it sloped upwards, which accounted for the lowness of the far end of the tunnel. As I went I thought it would be a good thing to follow my own tracks backwards and thus find a way out. The rock held the scent very badly, and as I was very used to my own smell I had a lot of trouble in following it.

Presently I came to a place where the paths met, and as I was determined not to go wrong again, I carefully noted all the distinguishing marks of the passage along which I had just come.

Then I cast around for my tracks again, and after finding them I wondered if these might be the ones that led to the stream or not. However, I took the chance, and following them up, I soon discovered that I was wrong again, and I felt quite lost.

SIXTEEN

AFTER wandering round and round the seemingly endless series of galleries and caves, and several times recrossing my tracks, quite suddenly I found myself at the entrance again.

The time was late afternoon, but I noticed that the sky was dark and I could not see the tent in the gloom which surrounded me.

I began to trot down to where I thought the tent would be about half a mile further, and as I went the sky became darker and I grew alarmed, for though I had been wandering for a long time in the tunnel, it was not nearly night time yet.

Then suddenly the wind rose, and a few flakes of snow fell in my face, and then all at once down came the snow. The wind blew a flurry of snow into my eyes and I was temporarily blinded, so brushing my paw over my face I pushed on.

I could hardly see a yard ahead, and the wind which was blowing into my face howled like an angry wolf, carrying away the sounds which I made to attract my master.

As I had twisted and turned so much in the tunnels I had quite lost my sense of direction which was usually so infallible, so after about twenty minutes struggling with the wind, I found myself at the brink of the precipice, still further from my master.

By now the wind had reached a terrible force, and for a little while it was all I could do to prevent myself from being blown over the edge.

Presently it abated a little, and I soon gained the shelter of a protecting boulder, and I sat down under the lee of it. The wind, however, returned with still greater force and the snow utterly shut out all the light, so I stayed behind the rock, but a powerful eddy of air kept covering me with snow, and if I had not been continually shaking it off I would have been buried in a very short time.

At length the day must have merged into night, but I noticed no difference, either in the light or in the fury of the storm.

Soon the snow heaped up in a huge drift on the other side of the rock, and at what I would judge to be about the middle of the night, the great drift became over tall and a small avalanche entirely buried me. I was almost suffocated before I had time to scramble out, and on doing so the wind raised me up into the air in spite of all my efforts to keep on my feet.

After carrying me a little way the wind dropped me into another snowdrift which had heaped up on the windward side of an even larger boulder. I burrowed through the snow to the other side, which was somewhat hollowed out like a shallow cave and gave excellent shelter.

The place seemed very familiar, and I wondered where I had seen it before – when suddenly I remembered this was the place where the tent had been, and looking round I saw the marks made by the tent pegs. I searched for the remains of a fire, but it was outside the little semi-circle of protection and was buried.

It was evident that my master had gone without me, but where, I wondered, had he gone – up the mountain? If so it was unlikely that he would survive such a storm. If he had gone down the mountain, sheltering among the smaller foothills, he might have lived through it; but then it would be impossible for me to find him. I thought of going back to the house if the storm ever finished, which seemed hardly likely.

It must have been nearly a hundred miles either south or west to my master's house. I tried to recall our route on coming up to the mountains, and all the different ways which we had gone in four days, sometimes going on trail after game, and more than once making detours round lakes, but it was too much for my memory. After striving to collect my thoughts and failing, my senses left me and I sank into a sleep of utter exhaustion.

I did not wake up until the middle of the next day. The storm had ceased, and I started up with the intention of joining my master at once, but to my horror there was no track or traces for me to follow, for of course the snow had obliterated all of them for miles.

As it was freezing, a firm crust had formed over the top of the snow, so if I kept my feet well splayed out I could travel about with ease; but I feared that my master, with his boots, would sink into one of the deep drifts and never be able to get out. I searched for the least clue of his whereabouts all day without success, as I was afraid of going too far from the camp site, in case he might return.

Towards nightfall I became aware of my extreme hunger, so when I observed a troop of wild goats and mountain sheep coming down one of the dangerous paths (which they seemed to prefer) towards me, I ensconced myself in a hollow which I rapidly scooped out of the snow, and when they passed I darted out and seized a small fat one, which I took behind a small rock and there consumed.

When evening was coming on the sky became threatening and dark, and as I feared another storm I went up towards the entrance to the tunnels and went in. I was determined not to get lost again, so I only went as far as the place where all the tunnels met, and there I chose a dark corner of the square.

To my surprise I found that the place was littered with a lot of dry ferns and grass, and there was a scent about the place which I could not recognise. I thought perhaps I had lain down here in my wanderings the day before, for the scent was very like my own, but on second thoughts I saw that it was too fresh to be mine.

However, I did not worry about it, but fell to thinking what a safe place this would be to live in when one got to know all the passages and caves.

Then I wondered where my master was, whether he were still looking for me or whether he had lived through the snowstorm. I feared he would not, for his skin even with all his clothes was scarcely sufficient protection against such severe cold. I also wondered whether we should ever go hunting again together, or whether I should ever see my mistress or the children again, or if I should ever play with the ball any more.

In the middle of all these melancholy thoughts, however, I fell asleep, and did not wake up until the next morning, when I got up, and after washing myself I went to the stream and had a drink. In the tunnels there was twilight all day and utter darkness at night.

I roamed all round and round the passages which honeycombed the mountain and soon found the exit again. At first the dazzling reflection of the sun from the snow quite blinded me, but I regained my sight and continued to search for my master.

As the hours passed without any signs of him, and I felt quite sure I should never find him again, my loneliness can hardly be imagined, for after a year and a half of his company I had got so used to his voice and presence that I could hardly believe that I was parted from him.

The great white stretches of pure snow broken by occasional bare rocks comforted me, however, and the exhilarating air of the mountains felt strange in my nostrils after the thick air of the plains.

Then I ascended to the very highest reaches of the mountain, and I thought I saw some smoke coming from far away to the south. But I was not sure, for a bank of cloud rolled in, obscuring my vision.

I did not leave the mountain for fear that I was wrong and that my master might return to the site of the old camp in my absence.

At midday I returned to the cave and I slept until night, when I came out, and after about half an hour I had a fat goat. After eating it I went down to the stream for a drink. I thought I saw another animal just leaving on the other side but was not sure, so soon I went back to my cave and presently went fast asleep.

SEVENTEEN

FOR the whole of the next fortnight I searched for my master, even going down into the plains, but I never found even a trace of him. Then I began to lose all hope of finding him and turned to hunting. I spent more time in exploring the tunnels, which I soon began to know quite well.

They consisted of two main caves, one above the other, each with a great many tunnels leading off them, and they were connected by one main tunnel.

In the top one there were quite a lot of holes in the sides which let in light, but they also let in snow and water, so I always lived in the bottom cave. Also in the top there were images of men squatting on great flat stones, which frightened me. Some of them had six arms, and one of them had an elephant's head, and they were all very much larger than any live men that I had ever seen.

On the sides of some of the passages there were some pictures which looked something like men, but I could not be quite sure. And in one of the tunnels which led nowhere there were a lot of skeletons of men, but there was no meat on them, as they had been dead many years and some of them were falling to dust. Often I thought that I saw a creature of some sort, but I was never able to catch it, and I did not think it ever saw me, or if it did, it never attacked me, so I did not worry about it, as there was plenty of meat running about on the mountains.

One day, however, as I was going into my cave I heard a growl from the corner, and turning in its direction, I saw a pair of green eyes staring at me, and in the pitch dark of the corner I could not make out what it was at first, but when it bounded towards me I observed that she was a snow leopard nearly as big as myself.

She appeared very thin and hungry, and evidently she was trying to frighten me away from the goat which I was carrying, and I saw that she was wounded in the right forepaw. Then she saw that I was no enemy and she made friendly noises.

In a short time we had made friends, and I let her have some of my goat. It appears that she had wounded her foot on a porcupine a week before, and had hardly been able to get enough food, as it hindered her running powers.

I think she had lived in the tunnel nearly all her life, hunting in the valley and between the first range and the main mountain. As I was feeling very lonely we played together, and in the morning we went out to hunt.

When she came out into the daylight I saw how beautiful she was, with her white coat and the black line on her ears which extended down to her forehead and made her look very fine. She seemed to know this and also admired my spots, and I saw that she had quite a lot of intelligence.

When we sighted a solitary sha, which was feeding behind a rock, I felt that here was a chance to prove to her how clever I was.

So pushing her into a snowdrift I set off after it. It sighted me sooner than I expected, so I gave chase, running at top speed, and killed it just in front of her. She pretended to be looking the other way, but I could see that she was much impressed, and I drew myself up with pride at my fine size and strength for her benefit.

Hearing no appreciative purr, in answer to all my fine postures, I turned and saw that she was sitting with her back to me and was starting to eat the sha.

I was justly enraged as I saw that she was eating the best part, which is, in my opinion, the shoulder. So stealing up behind her I gave her a sharp nip in the tail, and she relinquished the shoulder to me.

After this we went down to the lake, and I saw a red panda, who made off on seeing us.

Then she showed me a rock from which one could catch fish, and she tried to do so by crouching on the rock which overhung the water with one paw hanging down, but with no success.

As I had done this once or twice in the stream outside my first home I thought that I could show her how it was done, so I got on to the rock, and after waiting for some time I saw a fish. Then I darted down my paw to scoop him out, but I overreached myself and fell in, much to her amusement; in fact, the foolish thing made quite a noise, as if it was funny. I also saw the red panda on the other side of the lake looking highly amused.

Presently we went back to the cave where we slept. As night was coming on I woke up before she did because she kept grunting and rolling in her sleep, so for a joke I suddenly jumped on her and roared in her ear, but curiously enough she didn't see the joke, though it was very funny. She appeared quite offended and cross. Some leopards, I thought, can never see a joke against themselves.

Soon she recovered herself, and as one small goat was hardly enough for a whole day, we went out, and between us surprised a small troop of sheep and goats and secured a large fat one.

I picked it up and began to go home, but my greedy companion thought that I was going to make off with it and tried to snatch it away. I calmed her, and when we reached the cave I let her have the shoulder, to her very great content.

EIGHTEEN

FOR a year we lived together hunting in the valley and living in the main cave of the tunnels, and in spring our four cubs arrived.

At first my wife would not let me see them, but as I hunted nearly all day and night for food for both of us, at last she showed them to me. I have never been so proud and happy all my life as when I saw the four little cubs.

They were the most beautiful creatures that have ever been born, of that I was firmly convinced.

Their eyes were not open then, but I thought they looked even better for that. They could hardly walk, and as they went sprawling about they made the most delightful little noises.

Soon my wife drove me away, however, and as I did not sleep in the main cave for fear of disturbing the cubs, I went out into one of the side passages and slept for a few hours at a time.

I woke up suddenly with a sense of guilt, for I thought she might be wanting something to eat. So I went very quietly through the cave and out into the open. I encountered a large wolf, who was looking down the tunnel, but he cleared off as I came out.

Then I went up towards the big mountains, where I knew most of the game had gone. As it had been a very hard winter, which was continuing into spring, I had driven off all the goats within miles of the cave. I had to go farther afield, and recently a large wolf pack which usually hunted twenty miles down the valley had come up nearer to us, also some snow leopards. Both helped to clear off the game. So as my wife was very fond of bharal meat I had to go right over the valley for it. As I went I thought that if the spring weather did not come soon we should have to move our quarters, which might be bad for the cubs.

Presently I reached the usual path down which the bharals used to come to get to their favourite feeding-place, but I was forestalled by a snow leopard.

It was plain that he had not seen me, and by the code which my mother taught me I should have left them to him, but I thought that my cubs' health was far more important than that of the snow leopard, who had no family.

So I concealed myself behind a boulder and waited for the bharals. Presently one came along, and I thought that if I let this chance go it might get the scent either of the snow leopard or myself, so I jumped out, but it saw me at once and fled towards the snow leopard, who seized it and then stood growling at me. I thought for a few moments and then, seeing that he was not very big, I charged.

We closed, and the leopard, after a few minutes' struggle, managed to get a grip on my throat with his teeth and slashed at me with his long claws. But I got one paw under his head and I pushed with all my strength.

For a few minutes I felt the claws raking into my flesh, but then there was a ripping sound as the skin and fur that my enemy was holding gave way. His head slipped back and I sank my teeth deep into his neck. He gave a coughing roar and blood spurted all over me, and he fell to the ground with his limbs twitching.

Presently, when my fury died down, I became aware of the horrible pain of the cold on the bare flesh of my throat, and the blood streaming from the wounds in my flanks.

I was too exhausted to do anything, so I lay down in the snow for a little and watched the blood of the leopard flowing down the slope in many little streams, melting the snow as it went. I picked up the bharal and went towards home.

When I reached the cave my mate smelt my blood, but she did not leave the cubs, but she purred to me when I put the bharal down. Then she licked me all over, and after the pain had subsided I went to sleep.

In a short while the smallest cub began to crawl over to me and woke me up.

I growled sleepily, and received a sudden bite in the ear from my wife as a reproof.

NINETEEN

IN a few weeks my wound healed, but I had to hunt far and wide for meat of any sort, as the winter did not break, and even the goats went farther down to the warmer slopes. Meanwhile the cubs were growing and had opened their eyes, and soon they would be needing meat.

My wife was quite strong now, and she could have helped me only she would not leave the cubs in the cave alone, in case they would hurt themselves or get lost, or anything which she seemed to fear might happen to them.

They were going to be very big, and I hoped the spring weather would come before they wanted meat and got their enormous appetites, but it did not come. Every day I had to go farther, and stay longer, until sometimes my mate grew quite anxious.

Then one day the largest cub ate a piece of ibex and my wife felt proud of it. At first he sniffed it and played with it, then with a gulp he swallowed it whole. He choked and coughed as if he would burst, but he got it down at last.

In a few days the other cubs followed his example, and I worked myself to skin and bone in getting their food.

One day my wife came with me, when they were all asleep, and we got enough meat to satisfy their extraordinary appetites. They gorged themselves until we had to stop them.

But this was a lucky day, for on the following two days I was unable to get anything except one half-starved goat, and the cubs were quite unsatisfied.

Next day I went out early in the morning, and I went right across the valley to the lake, over which I crossed, as it was frozen stiff. On the other side I found a porcupine, but though he had tender meat, I thought I could do a little better than that.

So I went on, and presently I came to the bottom of the range of mountains which formed the other side of the valley, and they stretched up into the sky with their peaks hidden in the clouds. I went straight up, for I hoped to find a pass through which I could reach the farther and still loftier mountains, where there was sure to be food.

After the first gradual incline of the grassy slope I reached the snow-line, where I felt more at home, with the great bare boulders sticking up into the firm snow, looking as I thought rather like the ears of a huge panda. Soon I reached the place where the crest of the mountain could be seen, with its tremendous height thousands of feet above me, and I felt very small.

While I was looking up I nearly fell down a crack in the mountain side, so I proceeded more carefully, and I looked around for a pass, but I could see none, and it looked as though I should have to climb right up to the place where the peak detached itself from the main range. But this meant the loss of nearly half a day, so I looked very carefully for any means of shortening the distance.

The district over which I was now climbing was almost perpendicular, with many deep and dangerous ravines, and littered with many huge rocks, one of which started rolling as I passed by, as its base had been so worn away that the slightest push started it off. It gathered speed as it rolled down, taking huge bounds when it met other rocks, and on its way it moved many more, which went thundering down.

I watched them until they appeared no larger than pebbles, then I continued my course, thinking how like a panda's life was the course of the boulder down the mountain side.

At this point of my thoughts I nearly fell down another ravine, so I concentrated on climbing.

The cold here was intense, but I did not mind that so much as my inability to find the pass. Then all at once I saw about five hundred feet above me a deep cleft in the mountain side which would lead to the other side.

Soon I reached it and saw its remarkable formation. It looked as if the whole mountain had cracked and made a rift nearly a thousand feet deep. I quickly got through, thinking how horrible it would be if a rock got loose up at the top and fell on me. On the other side of the mountain I found myself on a gentle slope of snow going down about twenty yards before ending in a precipice of terrible depth beyond which there was a high icy plateau extending for miles to the north, and beyond that fold after fold of the great mountains as far as I could see. On the other side of the precipice I could see some ibex leaping from rock to rock.

I ran along to the place where the plateau joined the mountain and I crossed. Having stalked the ibex for the best part of an hour I at last separated one from the herd, and after a thrilling chase I killed it very near the edge of the precipice.

Being ravenously hungry I was just about to make a meal when I remembered why I had killed it, and picking it up I took it back to the pass homewards. Soon I reached the valley, and when I got to the lake I rested and looked at my ibex, which was very fat and no doubt tender, but I refrained when I thought of the cubs.

As I crossed the lake the ice cracked beneath me, but I was glad, for I thought the warm weather would soon come. I also saw some very small green sprouts on the banks.

As I reached the other side the wind changed, and I heard a distant howling of the wolves. I went slowly onwards and heard the wolves more clearly and thought that they had been lucky enough to get some big animal who was putting up a fight. I knew that only eight of the pack had survived, as all the weakly ones had been killed, and the remaining eight were the largest and strongest.

Then I wondered when the ice would break up on the lake, but my thoughts were interrupted by the roar of my wife. I answered, and started forward at a trot, then rounding a boulder I made for the opening of the tunnel, from which I could hear the roars of my wife, mingled with the howls of the wolves. Dropping the ibex, I rushed forward, and on entering the tunnel I saw what was happening at a glance.

The wolves had attacked my mate in the cave, and while five of them engaged her the rest were catching the cubs, one of whom was already dead.

With a roar I charged, and three of the wolves came to meet me. One leaped at my head, but I dodged him, and in a moment I had him by the neck and he died, but in the meanwhile one of the others had seized my leg and was pulling me down. I roared to my wife, and then more wolves heaped themselves on to me, biting and clawing wherever they could reach me.

I fought in silence now, and only managed to keep my feet with difficulty, as they kept trying to pull me down. I shook myself free, and then broke the neck of one who held my leg. But he seized my neck in his death-throes, and before I could recover the others swept me off my feet and another got at my throat. I could hardly move, but when I got a chance I struck into the mass of fur under which I was buried.

Once I managed to kill a wolf with one stroke of my back leg, as the others pushed him on to me, but the one at my throat hung on, though I clawed and bit him almost to pieces.

I could not draw my breath properly and my head swam. I regained my feet and caught an unwary wolf as he leapt up and broke his back with one bite, but with a rush they overwhelmed me again, and I felt bite after bite all over me, and I gasped for air, but the wolf at my throat never relaxed his grip, and there were black dots in front of my eyes.

I felt that I could hardly struggle any more, but then I heard my mate come back to the fight. She attacked them from behind and killed a pair of wolves in quick succession. This only left two, one of whom escaped and darted out through the tunnel, and the one who held my neck fell dead from his wounds.

I staggered to my feet, gulping down the air, then my leg gave way and I sank down, almost fainting from the pain.

My wife was hardly wounded at all, but the bone of one of my hind legs was broken through, and from a terrible gash in my chest poured out my life's blood. She sat down by me and licked my wounds, and soon the pain subsided.

I felt a growing weakness, and a beautiful sleepiness came over me. Then I saw three of the cubs come from the side tunnel. They were quite well, but the fourth, who was the largest, lay dead under the heap of wolves; but my wife never turned to them, and she licked me frantically, trying to stop the blood, which poured from scores of my wounds.

The light seemed to be fading, though I knew it was only afternoon, and I felt curiously aloof from my body and felt no pain.

The mist in front of my eyes was getting worse, and I heard the whimpering of the cubs, as if they were very far away, and my poor mate continued to try and stop the bleeding, but I felt it was useless.

My strength was ebbing fast, and I was weak like a little cub again. I looked at my wife, but I could not see her so clearly, and I thought of the eclipse and of my master, and I glanced up for the sun, forgetting where I was.

I looked at her again, and she seemed very far off and misty, like my mother was when I saw her in the hut years before.

Then a terrible pain shot through me, and when it died away I could only just feel her licking, and I sank into a wonderful dream, in which everything seemed far off, and I thought I saw my master, and then ——